Where Is My Frog?

We Read
PHONICS™

Parent's Introduction

Welcome to **We Read Phonics**! This series is designed to help you assist your child in reading. Each book includes a story, as well as some simple word games to play with your child. The games focus on the phonics skills and sight words your child will use in reading the story.

Here are some recommendations for using this book with your child:

1 Word Play

There are word games both before and after the story. Make these games fun and playful. If your child becomes bored or frustrated, play a different game or take a break.

Log rhymes with frog.
Very good!

Phonics is a method of sounding out words by blending together letter sounds. However, not all words can be "sounded out." **Sight words** are frequently used words that usually cannot be sounded out.

2 Read the Story

After some word play, read the story aloud to your child—or read the story together, by reading aloud at the same time or by taking turns. As you and your child read, move your finger under the words.

Next, have your child read the entire story to you while you follow along with your finger under the words. If there is some difficulty with a word, either help your child to sound it out or wait about five seconds and then say the word.

3 Discuss and Read Again

After reading the story, talk about it with your child. Ask questions like, "What happened in the story?" and "What was the best part?" It will be helpful for your child to read this story to you several times. Another great way for your child to practice is by reading the book to a younger sibling, a pet, or even a stuffed animal!

He jumped in the mud, and then he jumped on the car!

Level 2 introduces simple words with short "e," short "o," and short "u" (as in *get, hot,* and *bug*). All consonants except "q" are used at this level. Special sounds include "ck" (as in *lock*), "wh" (as in *when*), "ar" (as in *car*), and "s" as the "z" sound (as in *bugs*).

Where Is My Frog?

A We Read Phonics™ Book
Level 2

Reading Consultants: Bruce Johnson, M.Ed., and Dorothy Taguchi, Ph.D.

Published by
Treasure Bay, Inc.
P.O. Box 119
Novato, CA 94948 USA

Printed in Singapore

Library of Congress Catalog Card Number: 2009930802

Hardcover ISBN: 978-1-60115-323-4
Paperback ISBN: 978-1-60115-324-1
PDF E-Book ISBN: 978-1-60115-579-5

We Read Phonics™
Patent Pending

Visit us online at:
www.TreasureBayBooks.com

PR-1-12

Where Is My Frog?

By Paul Orshoski

Illustrated by Meredith Johnson

Phonics Game

Making Words

Creating words using certain letters will help your child read this story.

Materials:

Option 1—Fast and Easy: To print the game materials from your computer, go online to www.WeReadPhonics.com, then go to this book title and click on the link to "View & Print: Game Materials."

Option 2—Make Your Own: You'll need thick paper or cardboard, crayon or marker, and scissors. Cut 2 x 2 inch squares from the paper or cardboard and print these letters and letter combinations on the squares: b, d, e, f, g, h, j, n, o, p, r, s, t, ar, *and* ck.

1. Place the cards letter side up in front of your child.
2. Ask your child to make and say words using the letters available. For example, your child could choose the letters "f," "r," "o," and "g," and make the word frog.
3. If needed, you can present only the three letters, for example "h", "o", and "p," and ask your child to make hop. You can also ask your child to change one letter to make the word hot.
4. Try to make as many words that end with "-ed," "-ent," "-et," "-og," "-op," "-ot," and "-ar" as possible. Some of these patterns are used in the story. Possible answers include *bed, get, hog, stop, dot, set, sent, mop, jar,* and *far.*

Sight Word Game

Go Fish

Play this game to practice sight words used in the story.

Do you have *down*?
Sorry! You'll have to go fish!

Materials:

Option 1—Fast and Easy: To print the game materials from your computer, go online to www.WeReadPhonics.com, then go to this book title and click on the link to "View & Print: Game Materials."

Option 2—Make Your Own: You'll need 18 index cards and a marker. Write each word listed on the right on two cards. You will now have two sets of cards.

1. Using one set of cards, ask your child to repeat each word after you. Shuffle both decks of cards together, and deal three cards to each player. Put the remaining cards face down in a pile.
2. Player 1 asks player 2 for a particular word. If player 2 has the word card, then he passes it to player 1. If player 2 does not have the word card, then he says, "Go fish," and player 1 takes a card from the pile. Player 2 takes a turn.
3. Whenever a player has two cards with the same word, he puts those cards down on the table and says the word out loud. The player with the most matches wins the game.
4. Keep the cards and combine them with other sight word cards you make. Use them all to play this game or play sight word games featured in other **We Read Phonics** books.

and

he

is

down

so

my

no

the

where

Ben is a frog.

He can hop on a drum.

He can hop up and down.

Splat!

He can hop on my gum.

Ben can hop fast.

Ben can hop far.

He can hop in the mud.

He can hop on the car.

He can hop on a tent.

He can hop in the sand.

He can hop down my sock.

He can hop in my hand.

He can hop in a jar.

He can hop in a pan.

He can hop in a tub.

He can hop in a van.

Where can Ben be?

Did he hop on the sled?

No, he hops down
my back, . . .

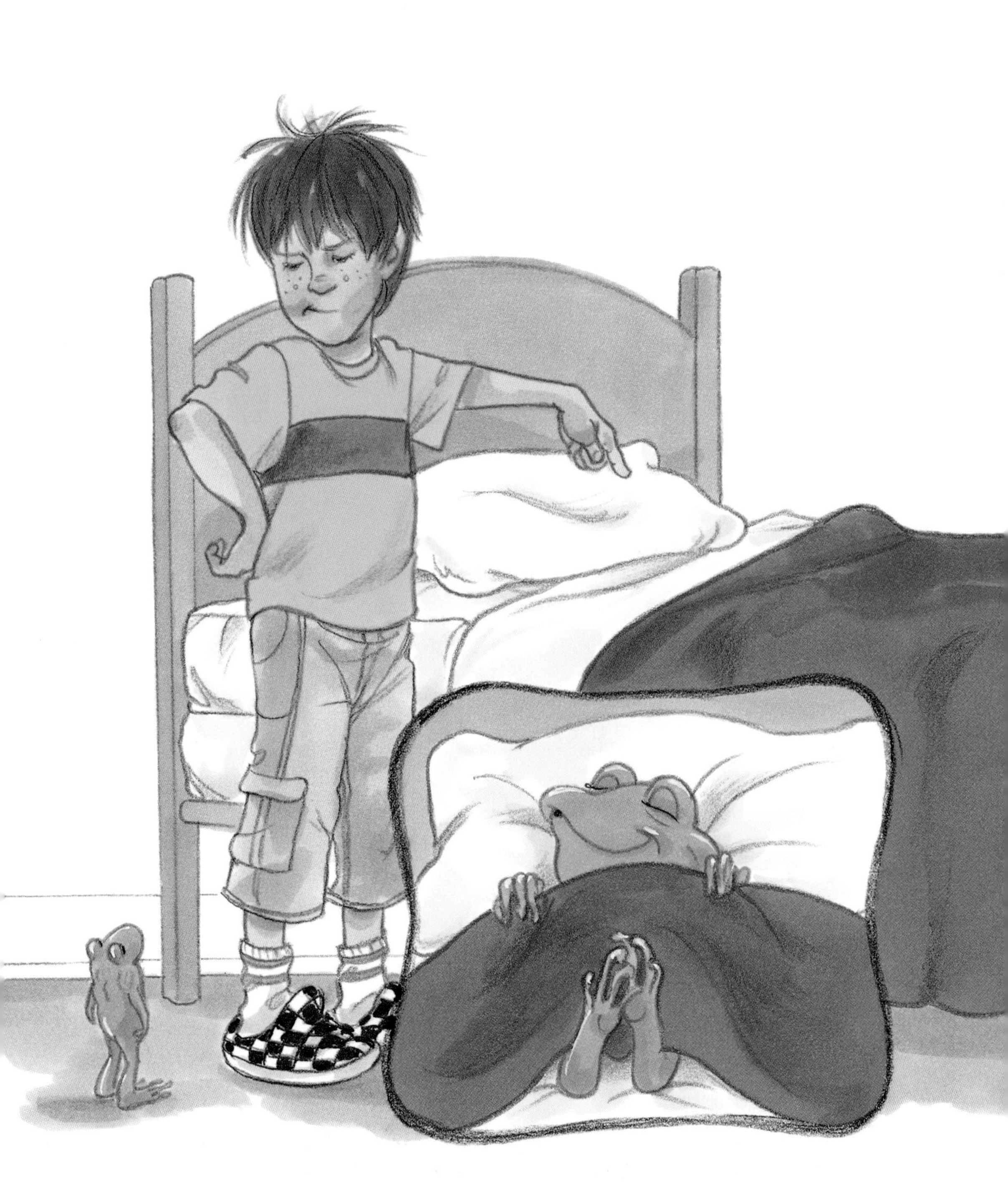

. . . so I send him to bed.

I Am Thinking

Practice with rhyming words helps readers see how words are similar.

Can you think of another word that rhymes with frog?
Dog!

1. Explain to your child that these words rhyme because they have the same end sounds: *frog, bog, blog, clog, dog, fog, hog, jog, log.*
2. Ask your child to say a word that rhymes with *frog.* If your child has trouble, offer some possible answers or repeat step 1 with other simple words.
3. When your child is successful, say: "I am thinking of a word that rhymes with *top.* What is the word?" Correct answers could be *hop, bop, drop, flop, mop, pop,* and *stop.* You might also accept nonsense words, such as *nop.*
4. Repeat with the following words:
   far (possible answers: *bar, car, tar, jar, star*)
   sock (possible answers: *block, clock, knock, rock, lock*)
   sand (possible answers: *band, hand, land, sand, stand*)
   hop (possible answers: *bop, flop, mop, pop, stop, top*)
   tent (possible answers: *bent, dent, lent, meant, sent, vent*)
   bed (possible answers: *fed, head, led, Ned, red, Ted, wed*)

Phonics Game

I Spy

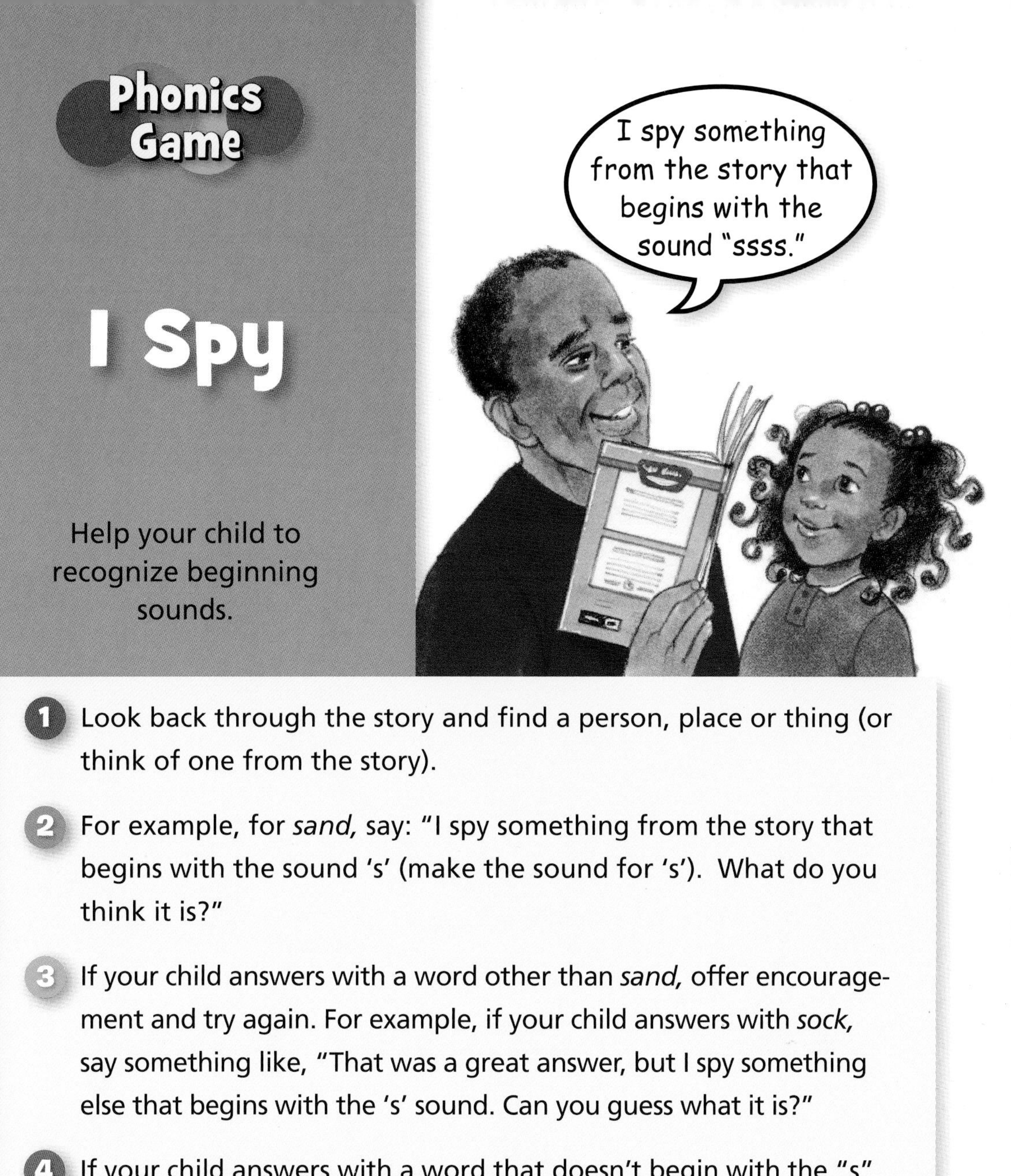
I spy something from the story that begins with the sound "ssss."

Help your child to recognize beginning sounds.

1. Look back through the story and find a person, place or thing (or think of one from the story).
2. For example, for *sand,* say: "I spy something from the story that begins with the sound 's' (make the sound for 's'). What do you think it is?"
3. If your child answers with a word other than *sand,* offer encouragement and try again. For example, if your child answers with *sock,* say something like, "That was a great answer, but I spy something else that begins with the 's' sound. Can you guess what it is?"
4. If your child answers with a word that doesn't begin with the "s" sound, offer some examples or possible answers: "*Sand, snake,* and *sock* all begin with the sound 's'. I spy something that also begins with the sound 's.' Do you think it is *frog, sand,* or *mud?"*
5. Continue with additional words from the story.

If you liked ***Where Is My Frog?,***
here is another **We Read Phonics**™ book you are sure to enjoy!

Bugs on the Bus

What happens when bugs escape from a jar on the bus? Find out in this easy-to-read story filled with flying bugs and a lot of fun!